To my husband and best friend, Scott,
who loves my cooking so much, he always wants more
– K. W.

For Tim and Noah, with love
– J. C.

First published in Great Britain in 2003 by Simon & Schuster UK Ltd
Africa House, 64–78 Kingsway, London WC2B 6AH

Originally published in 2003 by Margaret K. McElderry Books,
an imprint of Simon & Schuster Children's Publishing Division, New York

This edition published in 2004 by Pocket Books,
an imprint of Simon & Schuster UK Ltd

The text for this book is set in Adobe Caslon
The illustrations were rendered in acrylic paint

A CIP catalogue record for this book is available from the British Library upon request

ISBN 0743-47794-4
Printed in Italy
1 3 5 7 9 10 8 6 4 2

Dear Holly

To our special wee princess
of Tilly with lots of
love from Uncle Adam
and Aunt Debby
xox.

Bear Wants More

Karma Wilson

illustrations by Jane Chapman

POCKET BOOKS, LONDON

When springtime comes,
in his warm winter den
a bear wakes up
very hungry and thin!

He waddles outside
and roots all around.
He digs and he paws
fresh shoots from the ground.

He nibbles on his lawn
till the last blade is gone.
But
the bear
wants more!

Mouse scampers by
with his acorn pail.
"Come along," Mouse squeaks,
"to Strawberry Vale!"

So up Mouse hops
onto Bear's big back.
They tramp through the woods
for a fresh fruit snack.

The berries grow sweet, and they eat, eat, EAT!

But
the bear
wants more!

The noon sun glows,
when along hops Hare.
"Good day, friend Mouse!
How do, friend Bear?"

"I'm HUNGRY!" roars Bear.
Hare says, "Follow me!
There's a fresh clover patch
by the cottonwood tree."

They nibble on their lunch, with a crunch, crunch, crunch!

But
the bear
wants more!

Badger shuffles by
with his new fishin' pole.
"There's a fine fish feast
at the ol' fishin' hole."

They head to the pond
and they sit by the shore.
Bear catches fish,

but
he still
wants
more!

Meanwhile . . .
back at the big bear's den
wait Gopher and Mole
with Raven and Wren.

They bake honey cakes.
They decorate the lair.
It's a springtime party
for their good friend Bear!

Bear rubs at his tummy.
He smells something YUMMY . . .

and he still
wants
more!

Bear sniffs and he snuffles
as a sweet breeze blows.
He romps to his home.
He follows his nose.

His friends yell "SURPRISE!"
when he gets to his den.
But Bear is SO big
that he can't fit in!

Bear wails, "What luck! I am
STUCK, STUCK, STUCK . . .

in my own
front
door!"

Mouse squeaks, "Poor Bear.
He is wedged too tight."
Hare tugs, Raven pushes
with all of their might.

Badger gets a stick
and he prises SO hard . . .

. . . that Bear POPS out
and he lands in his yard!

Since Bear is SO WIDE, they party outside.

And he still wants more!

Bear opens presents;
he gobbles honey cakes.
He eats SO much
that his big tummy aches.

He snuggles in the grass
And he snores big snores.
He is full, full, full . . .

but . . .
his friends
want more!